THE TALE
OF
PETER RABBIT

THE TALE OF
PETER RABBIT

BY

BEATRIX POTTER

This edition is distributed by
AVENEL BOOKS
a division of Crown Publishers, Inc.

ONCE upon a time there
were four little Rabbits,
and their names were—
Flopsy,
Mopsy,
Cotton-tail,
and Peter.
They lived with their Mother
in a sand-bank, underneath the
root of a very big fir-tree.

'NOW, my dears,' said old Mrs. Rabbit one morning, 'you may go into the fields or down the lane, but don't go into Mr. McGregor's garden: your Father had an accident there; he was put in a pie by Mrs. McGregor.'

'NOW run along, and don't get into mischief. I am going out.'

THEN old Mrs. Rabbit took a basket and her umbrella, and went through the wood to the baker's. She bought a loaf of brown bread and five currant buns.

13

FLOPSY, Mopsy, and Cottontail, who were good little bunnies, went down the lane to gather blackberries:

BUT Peter, who was very naughty, ran straight away to Mr. McGregor's garden, and squeezed under the gate!

FIRST he ate some lettuces
and some French beans;
and then he ate some radishes;

AND then, feeling rather sick, he went to look for some parsley.

BUT round the end of a cucumber frame, whom should he meet but Mr. Mc-Gregor!

MR. McGREGOR was on his hands and knees planting out young cabbages, but he jumped up and ran after Peter, waving a rake and calling out, 'Stop thief!'

PETER was most dreadfully
frightened; he rushed all
over the garden, for he had
forgotten the way back to the
gate.

He lost one of his shoes
among the cabbages, and the
other shoe amongst the pota-
toes.

AFTER losing them, he ran on four legs and went faster, so that I think he might have got away altogether if he had not unfortunately run into a gooseberry net, and got caught by the large buttons on his jacket. It was a blue jacket with brass buttons, quite new.

PETER gave himself up for lost, and shed big tears; but his sobs were overheard by some friendly sparrows, who flew to him in great excitement, and implored him to exert himself.

MR. McGREGOR came up
with a sieve, which he
intended to pop upon the top
of Peter; but Peter wriggled
out just in time, leaving his
jacket behind him.

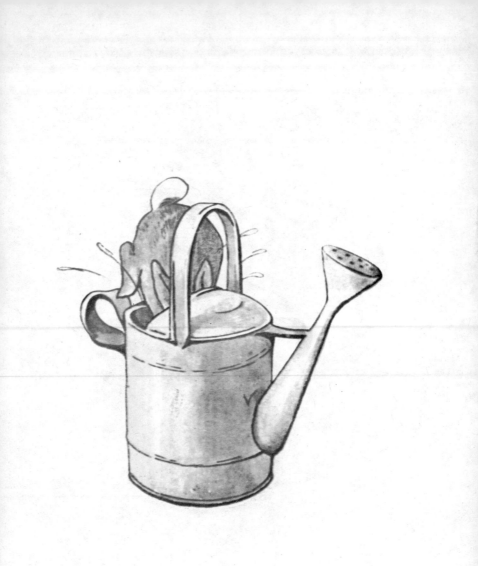

AND rushed into the tool-shed, and jumped into a can. It would have been a beautiful thing to hide in, if it had not had so much water in it.

MR. McGREGOR was
quite sure that Peter was
somewhere in the tool-shed,
perhaps hidden underneath a
flower-pot. He began to turn
them over carefully, looking
under each.

Presently Peter sneezed —
'Kertyschoo!' Mr. McGregor
was after him in no time. .

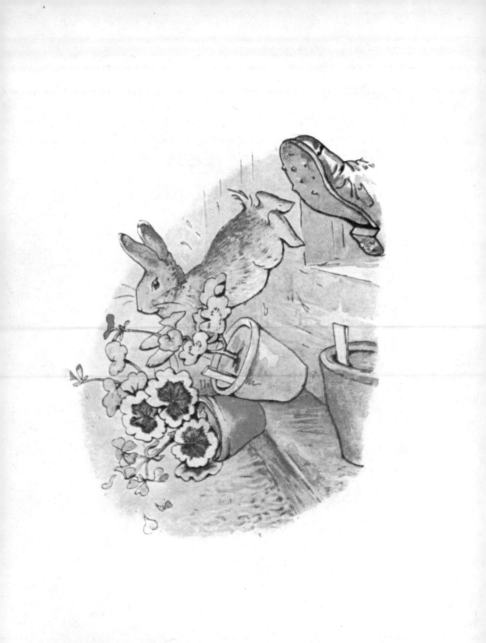

AND tried to put his foot upon Peter, who jumped out of a window, upsetting three plants. The window was too small for Mr. McGregor, and he was tired of running after Peter. He went back to his work.

PETER sat down to rest; he was out of breath and trembling with fright, and he had not the least idea which way to go. Also he was very damp with sitting in that can.

After a time he began to wander about, going lippity— lippity—not very fast, and looking all round.

HE found a door in a wall;
but it was locked, and
there was no room for a fat
little rabbit to squeeze underneath.

An old mouse was running
in and out over the stone door-
step, carrying peas and beans
to her family in the wood.
Peter asked her the way to
the gate, but she had such a
large pea in her mouth that
she could not answer. She
only shook her head at him.
Peter began to cry.

THEN he tried to find his way straight across the garden, but he became more and more puzzled. Presently, he came to a pond where Mr. McGregor filled his water-cans. A white cat was staring at some gold-fish, she sat very, very still, but now and then the tip of her tail twitched as if it were alive. Peter thought it best to go away without speaking to her; he had heard about cats from his cousin, little Benjamin Bunny.

HE went back towards the tool-shed, but suddenly, quite close to him, he heard the noise of a hoe—scr-r-ritch, scratch, scratch, scritch. Peter scuttered underneath the bushes. But presently, as nothing happened, he came out, and climbed upon a wheelbarrow and peeped over. The first thing he saw was Mr. McGregor hoeing onions. His back was turned towards Peter, and beyond him was the gate!

PETER got down very quietly off the wheel-barrow, and started running as fast as he could go, along a straight walk behind some black-currant bushes.

Mr. McGregor caught sight of him at the corner but Peter did not care. He slipped underneath the gate, and was safe at last in the wood outside the garden.

MR. McGREGOR hung up
the little jacket and the
shoes for a scare-crow to
frighten the blackbirds.

PETER never stopped running or looked behind him till he got home to the big fir-tree.

He was so tired that he flopped down upon the nice soft sand on the floor of the rabbit-hole, and shut his eyes. His mother was busy cooking; she wondered what he had done with his clothes. It was the second little jacket and pair of shoes that Peter had lost in a fortnight!

I AM sorry to say that Peter was not very well during the evening.

His mother put him to bed, and made some camomile tea; and she gave a dose of it to Peter!

'One table-spoonful to be taken at bed-time.'

BUT Flopsy, Mopsy, and Cotton-tail had bread and milk and blackberries, for supper.

THE END.